To Bobby~
Enjoy that
noble May!

Sarah Philips
402

recycled Jan. 2011
by Grandma

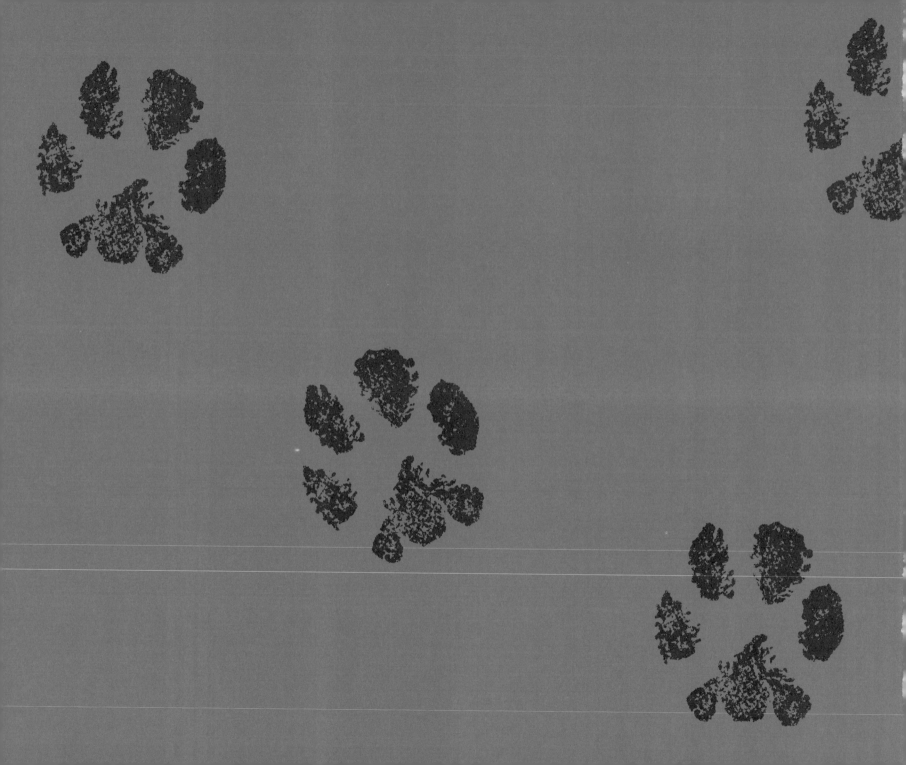

this Book belongs to:

_____

_____

_____

This book is dedicated to Elliot, my support my friend, my love. Thank you for making our dream a reality.

A company where children have a voice.

www.voiceofkids.com

Text copyright © 1999 by Sandra Philipson
Illustration copyright © 1999 Robert Takatch

Chagrin River Publishing Company
P.O. Box 173
Chagrin Falls, Ohio 44022

First Edition
Printed in the United States of America
10 9 8 7 6 5 4 3 2 1

Library of Congress Catalog Card Number 99 075233
Philipson, Sandra.
Max's Wild Goose Chase / by Sandra Philipson; illustrated by Robert Takatch
Summary: A naughty Springer Spaniel upsets the geese along the Chagrin River, and they conspire to teach him a lesson.
ISBN 1-929821-01-8 (hardcover)
[1. Adventure story–Juvenile Fiction. 2. Picture book for children–Juvenile Fiction. 3. Dog story for children–Juvenile Fiction.

Max's Wild Goose Chase

Max was a brown and white English Springer Spaniel who lived in a small town in Ohio named Chagrin Falls. It was named that because the Chagrin River flowed right through the middle of town, and as the river dropped under the bridge beside the Popcorn Shop, it created a beautiful waterfall. Max loved the Popcorn Shop because they sold ice cream there, and some little kid was always dropping his cone on the sidewalk outside. Max usually came away from a trip downtown licking his chops.

Now Max was a mischievous hunting dog. He got into trouble so often that if Max had been a kid, he would have spent a lot of his days doing time out in the principal's office or after school in detention. Some who knew him thought that Max needed to be in a very strict obedience school!

"obedience school
         . . . no way!" thought Max as he got ready for his daily "walk."

But, it was never a walk with Max. As soon as his leash was off, it was a run, a chase, and a hunt. In the woods and the river Max thought he was king, and he could do as he pleased. He was a Springer with an attitude.

Water from the river dripped from Max's brown and white freckled nose as he shook off from his first swim. As he was shaking, he suddenly heard a funny sound coming from the tall grass in Jackson Field.

"Ssst, Ssst, Max, Max,"

someone called.

Max ran toward the hissing sound to find his friend the black snake curled up on a rock, waiting for the sun to warm him up.

"You had better watch out, Max," he hissed.

"Why?" asked Max impatiently.

"Because Goosie Rough Rock is out to get you for chasing his wife and goslings out of the river the other day," replied the snake.

"Is that all?" laughed Max. "Goosie Rough Rock always has his knickers in a twist over something. I was just having a little fun with them, no harm done. Besides those little feathery brats of his are always in my way when I want to go fishing—swimming in their little rows, quacking at their mom for food, and being so noisy. They scare off my fish."

"I heard that Goosie is really ticked off. It isn't exactly the first time you have bothered them, Max."

"Oh, phooey! **What's the big deal?"** snorted Max.

The snake shrugged and grimaced, but Max was off and running in the direction of Goose Rock Beach, the hangout of Goosie Rough Rock.

Rough Rock, as his friends called him, was the **biggest, baddest goose** on the river, and most of the other creatures in the woods were just a bit afraid of him.

He had quite a temper and a reputation for picking fights over the smallest of insults. If Goosie Rough Rock was a person, he probably would have worn a black leather motorcycle jacket, a hat perched on the side of his head, and heavy black boots with silver studs on them. He might have even had a tattoo across his back that read, "Born to Fly."

It was well known around the river community that Goosie Rough Rock had no love for Max whom he considered to be a major pain, an irritating annoyance, and an all-round pest. Max was always barreling into the water and chasing the other ducks and geese just for the sport of it. Whenever Max was in the woods, the waterfowl were always in a tizzy, and this annoyed Goosie Rough Rock. He liked order, quiet, and a peaceful river with himself in charge. This latest assault on his wife and children did not sit well with Goosie Rough Rock. He was furious.

Max needed to be taught a lesson.

"But what kind of lesson?" Goosie Rough Rock wondered, as he headed for the meeting he had called at the Goose Lodge.

The Goose Lodge, an abandoned beaver dam on the far side of the river, was a place where all the geese got together to discuss problems on the river or just to have fun. This was going to be a serious meeting. As Goosie Rough Rock called the meeting to order, he announced that the first and only order of business was to think of a way to teach that

pesky rascal Max a lesson he would never forget.

Everyone had complaints about Max and ideas for revenge. Some suggested covering him with **crazy glue** and **sticking him to a tree;** others wanted to put **bubblegum** in his **kibble** or make him a reservation for the **smallest cage** at the nearest kennel.

Each idea was more outrageous than the next! What would work? Finally, after haggling for over ten minutes, Rough Rock and his friends agreed on a plan. It would take split-second timing and lots of strength, but it just might work. Four big geese, including Goosie's wife, Scratchy Rock, flew off to get the required equipment.

In the meantime, Max had been sidetracked on his way to Goose Rock Beach.

He stopped to sniff some fragrant grass and roll around on his back in some fresh horse poop. This last habit of Max's drove everyone who knew him crazy. Not only did he smell bad afterwards, but **he loved smelling bad.**

Every time he did it, everyone around would hold their noses and say, "Yuck, ick

. . . Oh, you are so gross, Max."

He just laughed to himself and ran on towards the beach.

As Max was rounding the corner, he felt something pull at his neck. He stopped short and looked up, just as a big vine from the oak tree had looped itself around his neck. Before he could shake free, he felt another vine tighten around his chest. He had run into

a trap!

All of a sudden he felt all the vines tighten, and he was being lifted off his feet and into the air. In a panic, Max looked up and saw Goosie Rough Rock, Goosie's wife, Scratchy, and two of their biggest goose friends with the ends of the vines in their beaks. They were lifting him off the ground, and soon he saw that he was flying over the river.

"Holy horse poop!" Max yelled.

"Put me down!!"

Goosie and his friends
just smiled, pulled up on the vines,
flapped their big wings harder, and headed for

... the Witches' Swamp.

This was the foulest swamp in all of the Chagrin Valley.

It was icky; it was sticky; it was black, and slimy.
It was full of bugs, biting fish, and snapping turtles.
It was thoroughly dank, rank, and disgusting.

Goosie and his friends thought it was just the place to drop Max for a little swim. "He'll never get all that slime off, and he'll be in big trouble at home. Besides, that place is really dark and scary and smelly. And, there are things that bite in there! What a pay back!" they all had yelled at the goose meeting earlier.

Max howled and yelled throughout his harrowing flight. Being suspended in the air by the vines was not comfortable, and he had no clue as to what was going to happen to him. Still, he didn't think it was going to be good. Making a lot of noise was about all Max could do, so he whined constantly.

"Guys, guys, what's the problem?

I'm just an innocent puppy! Whatever you think I did, I didn't do it. Look at this face. Is this the face of a criminal? Whoa, watch that tree top, you could scrape off my pedicure," Max implored.

After only a few minutes in the air Max was surprised to hear Scratchy say in her high-pitched squeaky voice, "OK Rough Rock, darling. We're here. Drop him on the count of three.

One . . . two . . . three."

Max opened his eyes just in time to see Goosie Rough Rock and his wife grinning at him. Rough Rock flapped his wing in a not-so-nice gesture as Max hurtled toward the ground.

The next thing he knew, Max was in the Witches' Swamp.

Ooooh the slime, the smell, the
muck and the mud . . .

it made for a nice soft landing.

Unknown to Goosie Rough Rock and friends, the swamp was Max's favorite place. It was full of the things he loved to play with, **water bugs, turtles, slugs, bull frogs,** and lots of **gooey, icky, black** and **sticky mud.** He could fish and swim around in this mud for hours, happy as a pig in its sty. As he heard Rough Rock and his goose friends fly off screeching with laughter, Max looked up. If the geese had been looking down, all they would have seen was Max's black slimy face and a great big toothy white smile.

"Thanks guys!"

said Max as he dove underwater for a fish.

Later that night at home, Max had to spend the evening in his dog house after his Mom gave him a bath with cold hose water. The herbal shampoo made him sneeze, and he was miffed that the geese had ganged up on him. Still, he had had fun in the swamp, and he fell asleep fast, snoring and snorting in his dog house. In his mind he was still

Chagrin's main bad boy and undisputed king of the Chagrin River woods.

let's write

Max is a real dog. What parts of the story do you think really happened?

What parts of the story came from the author's imagination?

Think up some other ways the geese could have gotten even with Max.

let's write

Max has adventures in the woods around the river and the swamps every day. Make up your own Max adventure story. (Hint: Max likes adventures that get him dirty and smelly.)

The Real Max and Annie

Max and Annie are English Springer Spaniels who live in Chagrin Falls, Ohio.

Max is two years old, or 14 in dog years. Max was a terrible terror of a puppy. He chewed pants and pillows; he dug holes and chased moles, and he never came when he was called unless he was real hungry. He was hit by a pick-up truck, lost in the woods in a snow storm, rescued when he fell through the ice in a swamp, pecked on by a gaggle of geese, and almost caught in quick sand. He is lucky to be alive!

Annie thinks he is a pain most of the time, but sometimes he has a good idea, like raiding the trash or picking the roasted chicken off the kitchen counter. She likes it too because he always gets blamed.

Annie is Max's dog big sister. She is 9 years old or 63 in dog years. She has always been well-behaved, well-bred, and well-trained. She was almost the perfect puppy. When she was twelve weeks old she chewed a tiny hole in the arm of the new leather chair, and later that week she spilled a whole bottle of pancake syrup on the kitchen floor. That was eight years ago; she hasn't done anything naughty since!

We know she loves Max because they sometimes "talk" to each other and kiss when she is in the mood. Annie is the boss of Max, but he doesn't care because all he wants to do is hunt, chase, run, swim, eat, and get lovies from the family.

In December, 1998, Annie had her left front leg removed because she had cancer. Read about her in the book, <u>Annie Loses Her Leg but Finds Her Way</u> and visit both dogs on our web site *maxandannie.com*.

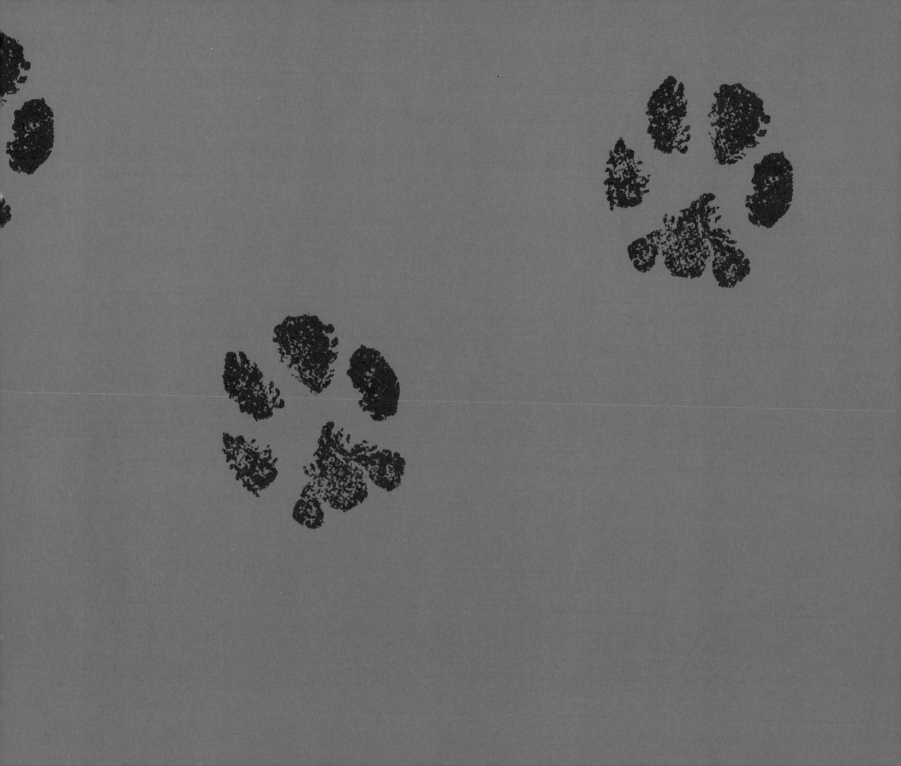

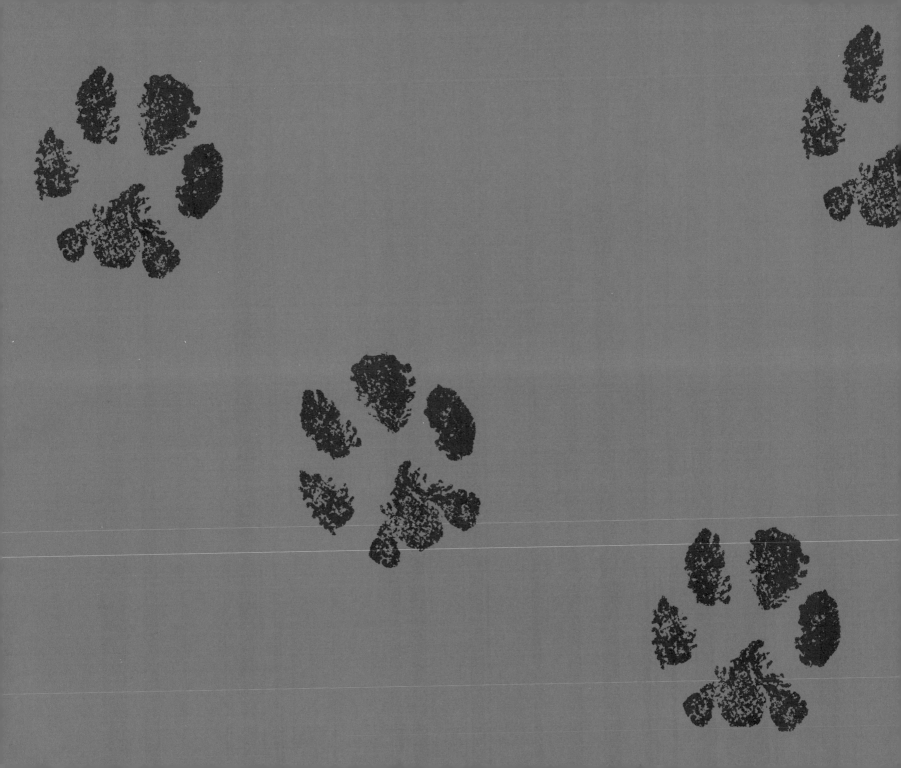